SOFT DAWN MIGHT EASE A MAIMED HEART

PRABIGYAN ARYAL

Thank you for being someone who constantly kept me like a secret until it maimed my heart. Eased myself at the end, knowing that the soft dawn of self-love had begun to start.

Art by Kritagya Poudyal (@kritagyapoudyal)

Contents

Acknowledgements

Never thought that I would continue ***'Wild Flames Could Burn Light'***, yet at the same time consumed by emotions until my heart got maimed and our sight got blurry. The brotherhood promises breaking and understanding that you cannot do anything but stare. This short story took a few long weeks while placed together unlike its brother; the first short story- Wild Flames Could Burn Light was supposed to start from the end and have a certain beginning.

But sometimes, it felt like the story ended with a slap. just like ours.

'Soft Dawn Might Ease Maimed Heart' contains so much more metaphors and honesty. The truth is spilled like water on the floor, yet it does not stain the fabrics of the carpet; for abstractness is filtered and the water pauses in the air with magic, love, hurt, and maim.

Before I thank you, I would like to thank Tejashwi Pradhan, Swikriti Tripathi, Mayush Shrestha, Chris Wardle, Chanda Prajapati, and Niharika Singh for always following my writing journey to the point they care not just about my art but also about me. Abin Gurung, Bishal Gurung, Anudit Shrestha, Sadikshya Sherchan, Anusha Singh, Prashanna Thapa, Bisheshata Shrestha, Tisha Dongol and Sanjeev Tamang (SNJV) were people who gave me space to talk about how I wanted to execute this story and a safe environment where I could speak about the things in my chest. My mother, who; without her, this book would not have been in your hands, and my father who although does not walk the same world with us, will always be happy for the smallest of achievements I achieve. Kaalo.101 family

(Helena, my eyes are on you too) who shaped me in a sense that they not just made me feel belonged but taught me that sometimes, we got to let things we love go to grow. Thank you Sezz, Seemron Rana, Manita Newa di, and of course; the artist of this book- Jharana Shreesh for the artworks that are in the upcoming pages of this short read.

Yashaa Bajracharya will always have a special part in my life because she introduced me to writing. Thank you Kritagya dai and Bina didi for being there with me at the times when I needed someone and last but not least, thank you, to you my readers and of course to you, the one the short story is about. Thank you for teaching me what growth is; spreading this light of positivity and self-love in me.

Prologue

He sits down with his feelings at the edge of the cafe wondering if he will get to see the rain slowly patter on the concrete ground. The sky above is turning dark and lightning flashes through the clouds. This is during twilight in summer days although they had met a few years back when apricity the sun provided was dim and wild flames had to burn to keep them warm. Many creatures hide during tough winter days and maybe by hiding, the angel he knew was securing some reminiscence that the angel never shared. But the secrecy, the hesitation, the simple slight actions from the angel made him realize how much he had been maimed. Now, here he sat, a cafe in the middle of a field; open spaces in all directions his glance ventures and sees; the blooming flowers, the greenery of the trees. Soft; the cool gentle breeze he feels in a land of beautiful sceneries. The sounds of rustling leaves and footsteps that came closer to him. He looks up and someone is already there sitting and smiling across from him. The once angel, the one he knew and respected to the point he sometimes felt ashamed; gawking back- putting up the pieces of the jigsaw puzzle; never knowing that abstractness and maim can go hand in hand. A book in front on the table and a watch on his wrist, words he shared and not knowing about the possibility if he will ever see the angel in the upcoming years again. Time; an enemy in the game. But at least, they have this sense of respect; the angel once kept him like a secret and in frustration yet with love, he filtered his words with metaphors and abstractness instead...

...believing that the color of this brotherhood love is golden for him, not the color of blood; red...

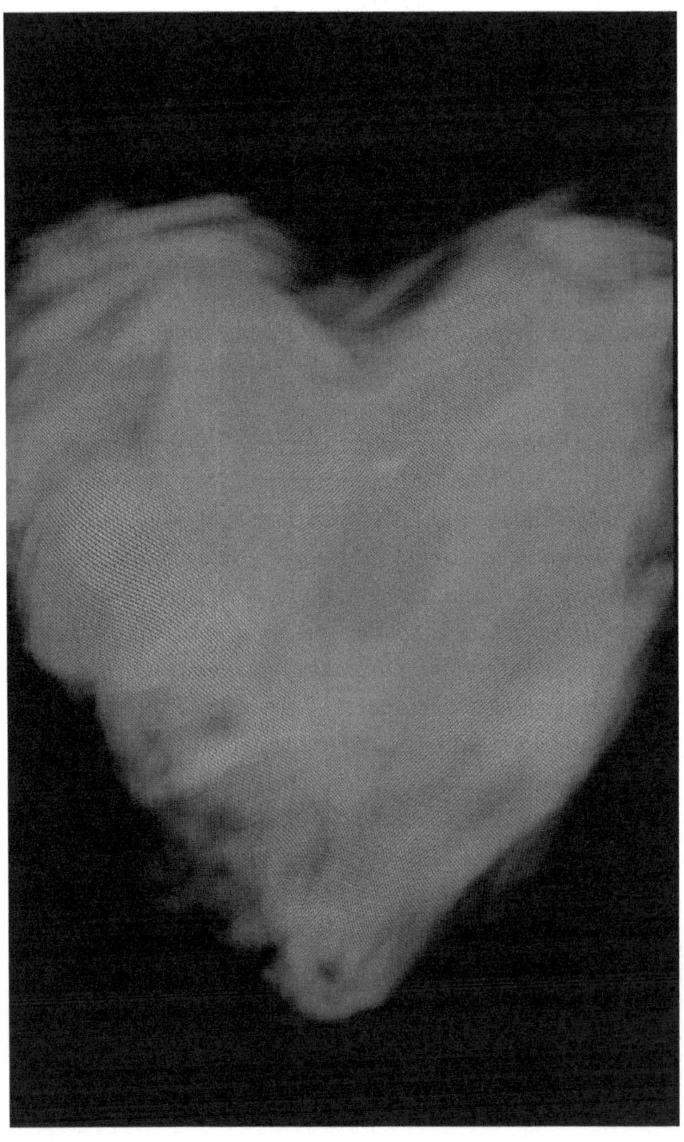

The color of brotherhood; Golden.

PROLOGUE

maimed

What can I tell you about us?

Abstractness. Sharing all too much and little at the same time. The beginning was happier now that the truths have been out. So where shall I start with this?

Maybe I should start by talking about love.

Something my father taught me to spread; why spread the unwanted expression when you can spread love instead? What is hate if you really think about it? Isn't it something you do that results in making your own grave? Actions always have consequences, don't they?

And I wonder if it matters what we think, trying to fight this pessimism in my mind to let serene tranquility come in. For after my father's last breath I felt broken and realized that no one was around. Even your shadow disappears sometimes when the angle for the light is exactly the right corner around. Shedding darkness instead of light...

Light...realizing that as I write about you; maybe I am painting a picture of you in. Lanky body with wings behind. An angel that fell from heaven, you were, in my mind. Dark charcoal hair and dark chocolate eyes, smiling with mischief and laughing without lies.

I sigh and so do you at times. Contemplating all the memories and cherishing them in our minds. Knowing that you came into my life when I was devastated, in a house party we met.

Wild flames burned our light that night and the new dawn of friendship rose up that time.

Now, let us leave the genesis, shall we?

Coming back to my senses and where we shall be. The future holds so much thought. And the present is devastating which sounds like a novel's plot, ain't it? But we all went through it. The past—the loss, the times that you and I met. Treating them like a secret game for we were hiding from plain sight, not because you were mine but more because of the crimes....

Forbidden moments we spent. Small mischievous misconducts we committed. Confessed that night and wrote about it; painting you with words rather than with colors, words; just like some scholars. Painting you with magic that has always flown from my fingertips, talking about how much you mean to me and spreading this love that my dad had always taught me. Your magic is different you see—unkempt and uncontrolled; after all your sight gave me magic to grow in me.

"I wish my father were here to see you," I had once said, but I never told you why. The reason was because you give me reasons to stay happy and euphoric to be alive.

Live, *instead of survive.*

For life was about making a mark, even a small love can impact a heart and that is something fascinating, isn't it? Something like art. In life, don't you find it hard to breathe sometimes? As if your chest is collapsing and the world is tilting and the beads of sweat that are dripping down your forehead and your neck make anxiety to kick in.

You were around to help me by listening to the beasts that screamed from my head; through my mouth, writing was tough when life felt upside down. But, you were still there and that made me feel comfort in senses I could not comprehend through words or sounds. You, can only be an abstractness that I describe, for the world is rough, you see, and although I was out of my senses when you once said you were confused about reality to me.

But that confusion faded in a snap. Awkward silence for so long that even the water froze touching the tap. I say that the end has ruined it. And in this present; it has ended, hasn't it? For I wanted us to be better than how we acted and how we had been.

"Not everyone knows the real me like how you have seen."

Time, wishing it would slow down for now, knowing that if I had asked you that question when we were in private, maybe I would have shouted, screamed, cried without glee. But even in that café, when no one was around. I let out silent tears after you made a groaning sound. Tired. Afraid to say your next words. Magic was at our fingertips, just not the way anyone would think.

"Will you remember me if I forget how to breathe?" I had asked.

Your reply was, "even if I did, I had to pretend I never had; this remembrance of you and I." What you did was you crumpled my heart and you threw it aside. I had given you my time and my effort and my love which I always projected and felt- thinking of you like a brother for years and you tore my love in a fraction of seconds.

Light dripped instead of blood, didn't it?

Hurt embedded in my chest and my knees wobbled before touching the dirt.

I cried, you stiffened; remembering that you left me first. But this is it, isn't it?

This is the part where you will be leaving me.

Yet, there still is hope in my heart that someday when I look at you; you will smile like before. The friendship will bloom in sunlight. But again, never knowing the possibility if I ever will see you, after all those situations and the plights we went through...

Because you flew.

I stayed.

We cared.

We both did. Maybe that is why I cried every night although such short time felt tough when you acknowledged every second that passed by waiting for that pain to stop and for that ugly screams to fall silent again; knowing that loving can hurt. But we now know that, brother; breaking is even worse...

...and that is how you maimed me first...

Reminisense...

CHAPTER I

Abstractness

"Abstractness; sharing all too much and little at the same time. Drifting across the vast blue sky until the world burned and so did our wings; stared at you flying close with a dagger in your chest until the world burned completely..."

I close the book and gradually place it on the wooden table. I sigh. "Those were the words I had written years back; when I thought that I had lost you, the light; the shine; the radiance in both our eyes. And I did lose you didn't I?"

He looks in my eyes just like how he used to before. No changes in his face although we were years apart. He does not smile; he only does when I try my best to crack a joke and it fails. I am not funny but dubious jokes that used to slip and the remembrance of him shaking his head slightly as if embarrassed and shameful for the jokes were not funny; they were secrecy.

But as of now, he sat across the table from me and behind him was a scene from where I saw the moonless sky; a night.

Just like those times...

Exposed to threat because of my vulnerabilities...

Consumed the friendship only to let things go.

"Maybe. Maybe not. What one's perception of loss might differ to the other, isn't it?" This time you smile, not a wicked one; but a gentle kind, almost soothing like a touch of a feather.

But the feather has long been burned.

Sometimes burning wild, sometimes the flames were just as gentle as the candle-light. Using words again to describe you, aren't I?

I wanted to stay in that abstractness, but now loss took chances in the abyss of emotions that I felt and which you; as of what I knew never did. Putting my emotions first on the table like a poker game and you putting yours at last; the end.

Endings does not always have to be in chaos or destruction, I realized. Endings can blow things out like the flames of the candle or like the snap of a twig in a forest somewhere.

Ends can happen in a clap.

Maybe an applaud or maybe the ending was a silent motion of goodbye. But again, endings can also be slow and lax. Yet, I could never tell how our story ended until it made sense to me now that I see you, here. Right in front of me...

Our story ended with a slap. Hard; on my chest—slapping my glass heart. Breaking was worse when you are tired to fight not just the outer world but also the demons inside.

But for now, let us focus on tonight. This time. Moonless night. Twinkling lights around the café arms. Your sight. That friendship. Lanky body and this time no wings behind. No burned world, in this café, only you, my brother, and me; the once fool who turned into a better lover; loving the world not just a particular person. For I had always been taught that loving was about giving rather than having expectations to come return and ricochet.

"Perspectives can change." I raise an eyebrow.

His face suddenly colored itself grey. "A lot has changed."

I sigh. "It has." Wishing I could hold back my tears. But the stinging started and so did the weeping and so did the cries.

"They say crying is a sign of weakness."

"Do you believe that?" Sobs. The line of discipline crashed. Even the grown man can let out beasts that they themselves unknowingly had been keeping. And maybe that was what I was doing.

"I do not know what I believe in." he sighed, truth spilled like cool water on the dry cement floor.

"I used to believe in you, brother." My lips quivered, yet I managed to say it.

Maybe he felt the invisible slap. The moment of the past we shared coming back.

A lot has changed, but isn't change important for the process of growth, for the process of recognizing our own emotional intensive tenses.

We felt.

But we do not feel anymore, now, do we brother?

believed

Believe.

A word with so much energy. So much positivity. Never knowing or maybe not acknowledging that even the pretty things have flaws, learning and acknowledging that believing *in someone can actually hurt.*

Remember? My knees had wobbled and touched the dirt.

Wings had burned.

Now, I myself cannot tell you if I believe in you *anymore...*

Confused in a sense that the words I say and write might not be cared about; for you told me to go all in, and here I am remembering...

...Remembering those fragments from the night we met. Tired to be in a loop; tired by yelling at the night sky, telling myself that I am okay this way; that some epiphanies sparked that day...

...and it has...

For I once believed in you, like a religion; I followed you. made a temple in your name and worshiped you...in the past tense, I even loved you. Took you as a brother while you looked at me like a member of a family you once knew. For you treated me like someone you cannot see, believed; that someday you would understand that I was only giving you this love for a friend and respect like a brother only for you to never acknowledge it. For pain was like cold water dripping down to the hot cement floor; soaking me dry with all the emotions I felt before.

Believed in you once...

...now, I do not believe in you anymore...

~

Sigh. I wish I could take the words back, and I am sorry for even thinking this way. Guilt tripped me, slapping me out of my senses. Sometimes I wish to take my love back; but again, I am not a person like that. I wish better for you even after the day I cannot breathe; remember, I asked you a question similar like this.

Sometimes when I sleep, I see all the black; wishing to paint them with golden colors not the flames that burned everything you and I ever had.

And when I wake up...

The light that pours through the curtains reminds me of you. the gentleness of the morning, the breeze, the leaves, the smiles before the heat of the rays becomes the unwanted treatment when I was your secrecy. Dare to say it our brotherhood was all just something you never even thought about, thinking I am speculating too much so I try to talk it out.

I know you too, not just the other way around. Smiled at you once, now all I can do is sigh, just like you do when anxiety creeps around. Believed and still do, your gentleness and your angelic halo and the reminisce of your innocence coming back in fragments...

The only difference this time is we started with happiness and kindness and feelings for a friend and I would not take them back...

...but the magic watch you gave me is broken now, stuck at the five; the dusk when we met. Never calling me once, for you were too afraid.

Asking you a question...

"Do you want to begin from the start?" *Again?*

CHAPTER II

from the start

"We started at the end, didn't we?"

A sigh. *I once believed.*

"Yes."

"Do you want to begin from the start?"

"If I could, maybe I would. But time does not work that way," you said.

"The angelic moments are up." I affirmed, stating the obvious. Still at the same café, staring at each other only to realize that there once were times when I gawked at you with love; a brother I thought, and although your vision blurred; there were times when we had shared that brotherhood bond.

Has it snapped? The rope that bind us, has it been tattered? Damaged? Cut loose by no other but you. The times when I desperately wanted to talk to you and you had blocked me for reasons that I understood. Yet, it hurt still; it affected me.

At times, made me into a perilous blind beast with actions that might tear us from between. Torn paper than a crumpled one, for the value of that paper is lost by tearing; the words vanishing in the enigma of the unknown. For we do not know when our story got told.

From the start...

Friend, you taught me lessons now that I look at the past. Enduring pain for two years taught me self-love at last. And although you did not reciprocate what I felt; you still cared with all your heart; I knew.

Now, for me that care is dimming like the light I see of you...

...I wish I could lie, but this is the truth.

Blurry visions that you see of me too.

• • •

The night is ending.

There is no moon tonight. Dubiously looking at each other; soaking in the details for the last time—until our eyes avert to glance at the dark sky.

Waiting for the sun-rise. The soft dawn of friendship to rise. Knowing that with those shades of oranges and yellows will be our last time.

Understanding that the past cannot be returned towards and whatever has happened, *has* happened; there is no escaping nor denying. Facts that made no sense sometimes, made so much sense later after you started to speak your words. Your truths, your tone; the news.

And although you loved to stay in the sincere serenity; I barked, you listened. I shed tears and you stiffened. Remember?

"Yes." You said as if you read my mind only to continue the conversation we were having before we both decided that to look at the night sky instead of each other.

Believing that if I looked at you, the ending will crumple and I have to love myself from the start, yet again—just the way the ground and hills had rumbled when the world once ended.

Remember?

Remember?

hoped

"I will consider you my friend no matter what." You once had said, spreading this warmth in my heart; hope, I called it—hope that once was, taking time to survive you. to let you go is the hardest thing I ever had to do. For we never wanted to ended up in this situation where we had fought. Verbally of course, disagreement is always a first. But again, you are not an ally, are you or are you not?

Both were angels once, now, we are nothing but a speck—just a single dot. The vast abyss of pain and the hurt.

When you said those words my mouth was shut, wanting to shred the paper that shows the statistics of the way you think and the ways of your cognition. Hoped that if I understood you better things would have been sought out. Hoped that if you came to your senses, you might have fought. Not with me anymore, but you know what I am talking about. The world is simple, but you make it complicated. Remember, it is your life, and whatever happens...

...I will consider you my friend no matter what. I will consider you my friend no matter what. A friend; a brother; someone who would have a bond even after the years that pass. Your childhood friend once told me that we both share this bond that they cannot comprehend.

Hoped. Stayed. Considered.

Contemplating whether giving chances again and again will make you understand the deeper end.

Now, your actions and your ignorance for my calls tells me to think new thoughts...

...making you a star whose light was so strong that it maimed not just my sight; but also my heart. Bright light pumped in my veins only for epiphanies to jump in this mind. Feeling like I lost something that I am trying to find.

"I will consider you my friend no matter what," happy when I first heard those words, wasn't I? Not yelling that although I am maimed, I always tell the world that "I am fine."

These times, I am not sharing the stories and opinions from my side, hoping that I will be able to leave you and love myself although there will be challenges that will arise.

"I will consider you my friend no matter what," you once had said. Hoping you have found out that from my side, although I cry and care about you and wish your life to be the best in the years to come; it will not be the same way again...

CHAPTER III

I shared

"When the world is in danger, what would you do?"

"We already went through that..." I said. "We were there when the world was crumbling and we could do nothing but stare. But it stopped and we rebuilt once, didn't we?"

He smiled. "yeah," his hand rubbing the back of his neck.

Sweat, dripped down my forehead, chest heavy to utter my next words I wanted to say.

"Thank you," I whispered, unsure if he heard. Lamenting the truths now, with abstractness, flourished the journeys that we took together and not so together for the secrecy were always your main priority.

"For?"

He heard, simple words, but attached with so much of care. Thank you for teaching me ways of self-love. Maimed me once, and I shared how too...

...maybe in some or the other ways, I might have maimed you too...

"For helping me save the world." I said.

"We were in this together."

I smiled, nodded; silent appreciation from a brother to a brother.

• • •

A cracked watch on the table, the book I had written about you, and something I had yet to reveal to him. But it was time to share. I fiddle through my pocket as it starts to rain.

The drizzle is soft at first, the clouds had been indicated me from the start all along. Lightning flashes in the sky; not purple but golden this time. A downpour starts to come, and I wish we could go to the shelter but we soak in patters of droplets and I keep what I was reaching for in my pocket...

"What were you reaching for?" you ask.

I sigh and take it out; a photograph; you and I; faces were unseen because I was talking about you with abstractness all this time, wasn't I?

He laughed. "that is us."

"It is," I said and pushed the photo at his side, although the downpour had soaked everything, it did not hit the picture of you and I. "this is for you."

I shared

I shared.

I shared

The photograph, the watch and the words. And with a smile, along with deep love for my brother, I shall walk away...

away...

this one last time...

The watch

blessed

*Blessed Blessed Blessed Blessed Blessed Blessed Blessed
Blessed Blessed Blessed Blessed Blessed Blessed Blessed
Blessed Blessed Blessed Blessed Blessed Blessed Blessed
Blessed Blessed Blessed Blessed Blessed Blessed Blessed
Blessed Blessed Blessed Blessed Blessed Blessed Blessed
Blessed Blessed Blessed Blessed Blessed Blessed Blessed
Blessed Blessed Blessed Blessed Blessed Blessed Blessed
Blessed Blessed Blessed Blessed Blessed Blessed Blessed
Blessed Blessed Blessed Blessed Blessed Blessed Blessed
Blessed Blessed Blessed Blessed Blessed Blessed Blessed
Blessed Blessed Blessed Blessed Blessed Blessed Blessed
Blessed Blessed Blessed Blessed Blessed Blessed Blessed
Blessed Blessed Blessed Blessed Blessed Blessed Blessed
Blessed Blessed Blessed Blessed Blessed Blessed Blessed
Blessed Blessed Blessed Blessed Blessed Blessed Blessed
Blessed Blessed Blessed Blessed Blessed Blessed Blessed
Blessed Blessed Blessed Blessed Blessed Blessed Blessed
Blessed Blessed Blessed Blessed Blessed Blessed Blessed
Blessed Blessed Blessed Blessed Blessed Blessed Blessed
Blessed Blessed Blessed Blessed Blessed Blessed Blessed
Blessed Blessed Blessed Blessed Blessed Blessed Blessed
Blessed Blessed Blessed Blessed Blessed Blessed Blessed
Blessed Blessed Blessed Blessed Blessed Blessed Blessed
Blessed*

Blessed us. Both of us—with certain epiphanies by which now, we will see.

Life is perilous alone, my friend.

I am just sad to see that for you; our brotherhood is a blur like the vision you see of me...

CHAPTER IV

Taking care: understanding that the bond was always there.

"So." I clapped my hands together and stayed put. The downpour was turning into a drizzle. Lightning flashed at a distance again, but there was no thunder. There was never thunder, for it meant wrath.

What does lightning mean?

Well, lightning was a symbolism just like everything else...

The flashes sparked a forest fire somewhere in my land; embedded the hurt that I screamed with wrath. Then only thunder decided to join in.

Lightning flashed at a distance; color the brightest golden ever seen; flashes of here and there and in between. Flashes of you, my brother next to me.

People ask me why this brotherhood is so important to me. The answer is simple, ain't it? Although the fights; we still try to take glimpses from each other's perspective and take decisions regarding that. Taking care, we were; for we understood that the bond was always there; truth it was, wasn't that? Forgot who you were in a time being; had expectations from you which was my mistake, that much I understand.

Life is about leaving a mark, they say. We both know we will not forget each other even after you fly away, leaving this shadowed burnt world apart.

The puddle near me, I see not just the golden lightning in the sky but it forms a world similar to the ruins we once built before.

Understanding that the ruins is not supposed to be built over and over; sometimes things just fall apart.

"So." I said again, "this is the reality, isn't it?"

He nodded.

"I am glad I met you, you know."

"I am too," he said as he tapped on the table.

The wooden table in front of us turned to glass. The things on the table were untouched though—the picture, the words, and the watch. The drizzle was still there even when the soft dawn was coming around. And as it rose, the sun; the beam of light. He smiled.

"Don't think too much now, take care of yourself..."

And with his words, he vanished into particles of golden light; swept and dusted off with the wind; the breeze that touched my memories.

There I was again, telling the world our story; telling not just the world but specifically you how much you mean so much to me; infinity. For you taught me that happiness is not relying on others or situations, but happiness is something you embrace; for it comes from within.

Burned world/ Puddle

loved

One smiles. The other sighs. One cries, the other tries; the best to make sure that they are still alive.

"Breathe," says the other while the one is man this time to sigh. The particles of golden and of light.

The magic that you gave still shines in my sight; I see things now, brother. Things that I was unable to see before. Things that taught me that happiness is not just being bubbly. It is accepting the things for what it is.

Loved you once, didn't I? I still love you as a brother, of course, I do. No matter the hurt. Hated to give you power over emotional stuff, things that I still need to comprehend for I do not understand.

Loved you, no matter what and I know you loved me back. Love doesn't have to be holding hands and stealing kisses, it can be simple glances with hidden heartstrings that play songs that you can comprehend.

Was confused about our bond for the longest time, wasn't I?

Thank you brother. Now, even if we go apart, you shall stay in my memory in a beautiful way. And even after everything we went through, I shall wish you the very best for the life you have ahead.

CHAPTER V

Till the world we know disappears...

I stand up. The rain has stopped yet the flashes of golden lightning still dashed. The puddle I saw still visible to me, the watch on the table which had turned back to wooden after you faded away.

Every time I close my eyes, I see the destruction we once made. The aftermath of the world burning in charcoal black and flashes of the light you produce.

The golden powers of this brotherhood. The watch that stopped at five, the time you and I met for the longest time. A feather; burning still, falling from the sky.

Taking care of myself now, for you have disappeared. And I shall love still...

...till the world we know disappears...

I walk towards the warden of the café and ask, "how much was it?"

"For the cigarettes or the viewing?"

"Both."

"Same price, fifteen rupees."

I pay and watch the puddle for the last time, then the book, then the watch and finally the photograph and walk into the soft butter light of the dawn awaiting me.

Till the world we know disappears...

Brotherhood lightning

Author's Note

Viewing: *To look at something before saying goodbye*

Confusion has been a big part of writing this nonfiction mixed with mythical prose.

I have shared everything I had wanted to in an abstract way in this and previous short reads. All I know is that my friend left a permanent mark on understanding and what it means to be alive and happy. He taught me what living means, and for that; I am forever grateful. Thank you brother.

Also By Prabigyan Aryal

IF SHADOWS COULD TALK SERIES:

1. HIS AFFLICTED MIND
2. ASHVALE
3. OUR BROKEN UNIVERSE (with MAYUSH SHRESTHA) *coming soon...*

SHORT STORIES:

1. Wild Flames Could Burn Light
2. Soft Dawn Might Ease Maimed Heart

About The Author

21-year-old Prabigyan Aryal (he/him) believes that everyone in this world has stories to tell and that we all are storytellers. Before he began bleeding his imagination onto paper, he used to think a lot about people, situations and emotions. His journey of writing began when he was in grade seven after he realized that the world he comes up with can actually be written down in a form of art. He started writing stories ever since. Aryal's debut book, *His Afflicted Mind,* is a narration of how a depressed mind sees life. He wrote his first book as a journal before telling a story, as he was going through the same emotions and feelings he portrayed in the book. However, Aryal wanted *Ashvale* to be the light that we see during twilight in a town filled with memories—in a town with differences in changes between people, love and death. These short stories; *Wild Flames Could Burn Light* and *Soft Dawn Might Ease A Maimed Heart* are again, fiction mixed with non-fiction emotions.

(Instagram Account: @prabigyanaryal)

Prabigyan Aryal

About The Illustrator

Jharana Shreesh (she/her) is a queer-identifying individual who enjoys making queer art (something that has given her a way to express herself), watching queer shows or having a concert of her own. Art; for her is the only thing that makes her lose track of time. She believes she is in the process of learning new things as we take one step at a time.

(Instagram account; @shreeshjharana)

Jharana Shreesh

Printed by Libri Plureos GmbH in Hamburg,
Germany